SPANISH-ENGLISH GLOSSARY

adiós
(ah-dee-OS): good-bye

amigo
(ah-MEE-goh): friend

bravo!
(BRAH-vo): excellent!

buenos días
(BWAY-noss DEE-as): good day

cielito lindo
(see-eh-LEE-toe LEEN-dough): pretty little darling

de
(day): of

el or **la**
(el) or (la): the

estrellita
(ess-tray-YEE-ta): little star

fábrica de vídrio
(FAB-ree-cah day vee-DREE-oh): glass factory

golondrina
(go-lon-DREE-nah): swallow (bird)

grande
(GRAHN-day): big

harina
(ar-EEN-ah): flour

luna
(LOON-ah): moon

mariposa
(mar-ee-POS-ah): butterfly

marcha
(MAR-chah): march

Mejico
(MEH-hee-co): Mexico

mi
(mee): my

muchacho
(moo-CHA-cho): boy

por favor
(pour fah-VOR): please

qué bonita!
(kay boh-NEE-tah): how pretty!

qué pasa?
(kay PAH-sah): what's going on?

señor
(sen-YOR): mister

sí
(see): yes

sol
(saul): sun

sombrero
(som-BRER-oh): hat

tortilla
(tor-TEE-ya): pancake

For Lyn —C. G.

To my mother, who taught me to fight for my dreams —A. J.

Atheneum Books for Young Readers ★ An imprint of Simon & Schuster Children's Publishing Division ★ 1230 Avenue of the Americas, New York, New York 10020 ★ Text copyright © 2004 by Campbell Geeslin ★ Illustrations copyright © 2004 by Ana Juan
The illustrations for this book are rendered in acrylic and crayons. ★ Manufactured in China ★ First Edition ★ 10 9 8 7 6 5 4 3 2 1
Library of Congress Cataloging-in-Publication Data ★ Geeslin, Campbell. ★ Elena's serenade / Campbell Geeslin ; illustrated by Ana Juan. —1st ed. ★ p. cm. ★ "An Anne Schwartz Book." ★ Summary: In Mexico, a little girl goes on a journey to learn to be a glassblower and gains confidence along the way. ★ ISBN 0-689-84908-7 ★ [1. Glassblowing and working—Fiction. 2. Fathers and daughters—Fiction. 3. Sex role—Fiction. 4. Mexico—Fiction.] I. Juan, Ana, ill. II. Title. ★ PZ7.G25845 El 2004 ★ [E]—dc21 ★ 2002003233

ELENA'S SERENADE

WRITTEN BY

campbell geeslin

ILLUSTRATED BY

ana juan

An Anne Schwartz Book
Atheneum Books for Young Readers
New York ★ London ★ Toronto ★ Sydney ★ Singapore

In Mexico the sun is called *el sol,* and the moon is called *la luna.* I am called Elena.

My papa is a glassblower. He puffs out his cheeks, blows into a long pipe, and a bottle appears at the other end, just like magic.

One afternoon I find an old pipe of Papa's. I ask him if he will teach me to be a glassblower too, but he shakes his head. "You are too little, Elenita, and the hot glass might burn you. Besides, who ever heard of a girl glassblower?"

Even though I am as mad as a wet hen, I don't let Papa see my tears.

When I get home, my brother Pedro asks, "Why the sad face, Elena?"

"I want to blow glass, but Papa says I'm too little and anyway, who ever heard of a girl glassblower?"

"Monterrey is where the great glassblowers are," Pedro says. "You should go there."

Should I? I'm scared to leave Papa, but maybe I *should*.

The next morning I borrow a pair of Pedro's trousers, hide my hair under his old *sombrero,* and set out. Since girls aren't supposed to be glassblowers, I'll pretend that I am a boy.

El sol blazes like Papa's furnace, and the road is long. I get hotter and hotter until, at last, I must rest. To pass the time, I puff out my cheeks and blow on my pipe. What is that? A pretty sound comes out!

Ever so gently I blow again. The notes get higher, *pree-tat-tat, pree-tat-tat*. I can hardly believe my ears—my pipe is making music!

I blow, easy and then harder, *pree-tat-tat,* until I find all the notes for a happy song called "Burro Serenade." I make the music go *clip-clop, clip-clop,* just the way a burro trots along.

♪ clip-clop ♪ clip-clop ♪

Over and over I play the tune, my heart flying higher with every note. At last there are no mistakes.

From behind a cactus Burro trots up and says, "Oh, *señor*, I was lost and lonely until I heard my song. Now I am smiling, see? May I take you someplace?"

"*Sí*," I say. "I am on my way to Monterrey to learn to be a glassblower."

"If you can make music, I'm sure you can make glass," Burro says. I climb on his back, and off we go.

It is almost evening when we overtake Roadrunner, limping along. "Oh, *Señor* Roadrunner," I say, "you are supposed to fly like the wind. *Qué pasa?*"

Roadrunner sighs. "I might as well be a turtle. Every time I try to run, one of my legs forgets how. Even a rock can go faster."

"Let's try this," I say. "I will blow my pipe slowly, and you step along with the music." I wonder if the steady beat of *"La Marcha Grande de Mejico"* will help. I sound out the notes until I have it just right.

Roadrunner's limp changes to a march. "Oh, that music makes me proud to be a Mexican!" he exclaims.

TUM, tum, TUM, tum. I play faster like a drum. *TUMtumTUMtumTUMtum.*

Suddenly, Roadrunner surges ahead. "Where are you going?" he calls back to me.

"I am on my way to Monterrey to learn to be a glassblower!" I shout.

"You play such a fine march, certainly you'll make a fine glassblower." His voice fades away as he disappears in a cloud of dust.

That evening, after *la luna grande* has risen, Burro lies down and I use him as a pillow. We have traveled all day, and we are tired. As I drift off to sleep, I think of home.

Sometime during the night I am awakened by awful howling. *La luna grande* is high in the sky and the desert is golden. Coyote runs toward us, chased by an owl, two bats, and a lizard who are hurling rocks at him.

"*Qué pasa, Señor* Coyote?" I ask.

His tongue hangs out and he puffs and puffs. "When *la luna* is bright, I sing—I can't help myself. But everyone hates my song."

"Let me hear you," I say.

Coyote throws back his head. *"Ouchowahooooo!"* he howls.
"Ay yah!" I cry.
The owl hoots, the bats shriek, and the lizard covers his ears.

"Listen to this," I say, "and sing along." I take my pipe and blow, very softly, a low note. It is the beginning of a song my papa used to sing to me, *"Cielito Lindo."*

"Hmmm, that sounds sweet as honey," Coyote says. "Let me try." He clears his throat and begins, "For when our hearts sing together, *ci-e-li-to lin-do,* love comes along . . ." His voice is soft and low.

"Bravo!" I shout.

"Bravo!" cry the owl, the bats, and the lizard.

The happy Coyote asks me where I am going. "I am on my way to Monterrey to become a glassblower."

"If you could teach me to sing, you can do anything!" he declares.

Then, as Coyote sings his sweet love song to *la luna,* Burro and I slip back into sleep.

Next morning, Burro and I start off with the sunrise, and at last we get to Monterrey. There are many houses and buildings and everyone is in a hurry. Before me is a factory where the furnace's giant mouth is full of bubbling glass.

"*Adiós, mi amigo,*" I say to Burro, and then step inside.

In front of me, four big men stand stiff as soldiers, puffing on long pipes. As their balloon cheeks shrink, glass bubbles appear and turn into tall bottles, medium bottles, and tiny bottles.

"What do you want?" their boss yells at me.

I cough and in a low voice I say, "*Por favor, señor . . .* I want to be a glassblower."

The men laugh. The boss winks and says, "Okay, *muchacho*. Let's see what you can do."

I twirl the end of my pipe in the hot glass just the way Papa does.

What is going to happen?

I close my eyes and gulp a deep breath. I puff out my cheeks and begin to play a song called *"Estrellita,"* about a little star.

When the men hear music, they laugh even harder. I think they will never stop, but then . . .

I remember how my pipe helped Burro, how it helped Roadrunner and Coyote. I blow, strong and steady, and when I open my eyes, I have made a star!

The men's mouths drop open in surprise.

I tap the star off into the sand to cool, and then I play *"Estrellita"* again. At the end of my pipe another glass star bursts out.

The men try to blow music too, but only burping noises and crooked bottles
come from their pipes.

"Welcome, little glassblower!" the boss says, and shakes my hand. He puts my
stars in the factory windows where they twinkle like real stars.

As soon as the children in Monterrey see them, they all want one. The stars sell
faster than I can blow them.

One night, when I am working alone, I get tired of playing *"Estrellita."* I twirl a huge glass glob on to the end of my pipe and begin a song called *"La Golondrina."* It is about a swallow gliding over the sea.

A glass bird appears. As I play, its wings grow long. I play on, and it becomes the size of Roadrunner. I take a quick breath to play more, and the glass bird grows as big as Coyote. I blow and blow, and my swallow becomes bigger than Burro.

I tap the bird off and the glass cools. The swallow's great wings stretch from one wall to the other.

Oh, I wish Papa could see what I can do!

After sliding open the factory's big back door, I push my bird out into the alley. I climb on and play *"La Golondrina"* again. Slowly the swallow rises into the air.

I'm flying! Down below, the lights shine from hundreds of windows with glass stars in them.

As I play my pipe the bird flies higher. I turn south, and when I see my town below, I play softer and softer and finally stop. The bird glides down onto a field of lilies. I run home, climb in the window, and curl up in my own little bed.

The next morning, when Papa goes off to work, I get up. I have a plan all figured out. I put on Pedro's pants and *sombrero* again, and then I tear a *tortilla* in half and paste it on to my chin with flour and water.

I take my pipe and run straight to Papa's factory.

"*Buenos días, señor,*" I say, in an old man's shaky voice. "I am a glassblower, come all the way from Monterrey."

"Why, grandfather," Papa says politely, "you aren't as tall as your pipe. How can you blow glass?"

I twirl hot glass on to the end and begin to play a song called *"La Mariposa,"* about how pretty butterflies are. A glass butterfly floats from my pipe and flutters about, its wings chiming.

"*Qué bonita!*" Papa exclaims. "If only my daughter were here to see this."

"But she is!" I shout, and rip off my *tortilla* beard and toss the *sombrero* in the air.
"Is that you, Elena?" Papa asks, squinting.

"At your service, Papa," I reply and laugh. Then I tell him about all the funny and amazing things that happened on my trip to Monterrey.

Now every day Papa and I work side by side at our great furnace. Papa blows bottles and pitchers and drinking glasses. I blow birds, stars, butterflies, and songs.

On Saturdays tourists come from all over to dance to the music and to try to catch a glass butterfly. If you close your eyes and sit absolutely still, you may hear their wings chiming like little glass bells. Listen . . .